With special thanks to the
SpongeBob SquarePants writers

Stephen Hillenburg

Based on the TV series *SpongeBob SquarePants*®
created by Stephen Hillenburg as seen on Nickelodeon®

SIMON SPOTLIGHT
An imprint of Simon & Schuster Children's Publishing
Division
1230 Avenue of the Americas
New York, New York 10020

Manufactured in the United States of America

2 4 6 8 10 9 7 5 3
ISBN 0-689-85175-8

Greetings From Bikini Bottom

Simon Spotlight/Nickelodeon

New York   London   Toronto   Sydney   Singapore

Bubble Blowing Is Serious Business in Bikini Bottom

1 First we go like this ... spin around!

2 Double-take three times ... one, two, and three, then ...

3 Pelvic thrust — Whoo-oooo-whoo!

4 Stomp on your right foot. Don't forget it!

5 Now it's time to bring it around town. Go ahead, BRING IT AROUND TOWN!

6 Then you do this, then this, then this, and this and that and thisandthatandthisandthatandthisandthat!

Go, SpongeBob!
Go, SpongeBob!
Go, self!

PATRICK and SPONGEBOB

Man Sponge and Boy Patrick!
To the invisible boatmobile!

SPONGEBOB: WAIT! I don't have a license.
PATRICK: Well, this is an invisible boat ... so you need an invisible license!
SPONGEBOB: You're the best sidekick ever.

SQUIDWARD TENTACLES

Oh, my aching tentacles!

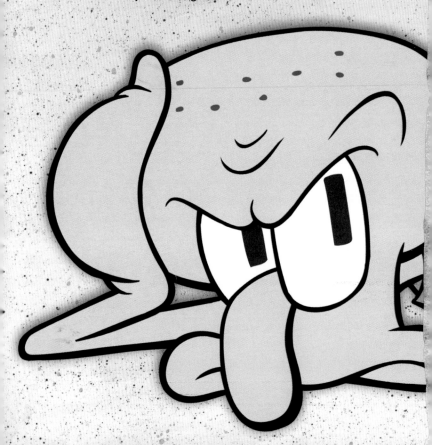

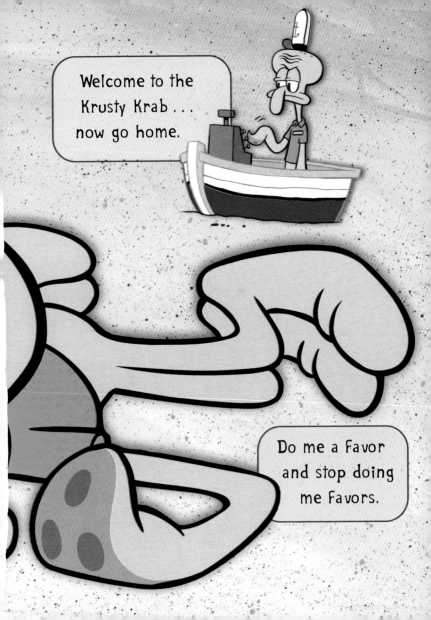

GARY

Meow.

Meow?

MEOW!

SANDY: I like you, SpongeBob. We could be tighter than bark on a tree.

SPONGEBOB: I like you, too, Sandy. Say, what's that thing on your head?

MR. KRABS

Do you smell it? I smell the smelly smell of something that smells smelly.

Ahh, it warms my wallet to see my employees coming in early.

Attention! All Krusty Krab employees— attention! Get the anchors out of your pants and report to my office! That will be all.

Who stole the Krabby Patty?

Clues:
1. Has a tough time picking out glasses
2. Is in the restaurant business
3. Is a college graduate
4. Evil

Wherever there is a secret recipe, there is someone who wants to steal it. . . .

PLANKTON

It's becoming increasingly
obvious. I can deny it no
longer... I am small.

Oh, Bikini Bottom, we pledge our hearts to you. As faithful, as deep, as true, as blue, oh, Bikini Bottom, we love you!